No Way Yirrikipayi!

By children from Milikapiti School, Melville Island,
with Alison Lester

INDIGENOUS LITERACY FOUNDATION

Yirrikipayi was hungry
so he went hunting.

Yirrikipayi – Crocodile

He surprised a Jarrakarlani on the reef
but the Jarrakarlani said,
'No way, Yirrikipayi!
You're not eating me today.
I've got a hard shell,
it'll make you unwell.'

Jarrakarlani - Turtle

He went for a Kirluwarringa in the shallows
but the Kirluwarringa said,
'No way, Yirrikipayi!
You're not eating me today.
The spear in my tail
will cause you to wail.'

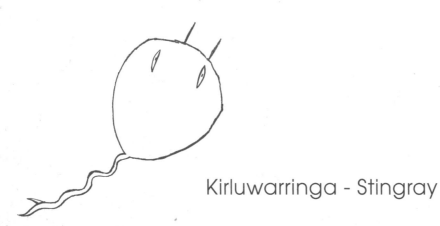

Kirluwarringa - Stingray

Yirrikipayi was getting hungrier and hungrier.

He chased a Marntuwunyini over the seagrass
but the Marntuwunyini said,
'No way, Yirrikipayi!
You're not eating me today.
My whiskery nose
will tickle your toes.'

Marntuwunyini - Dugong

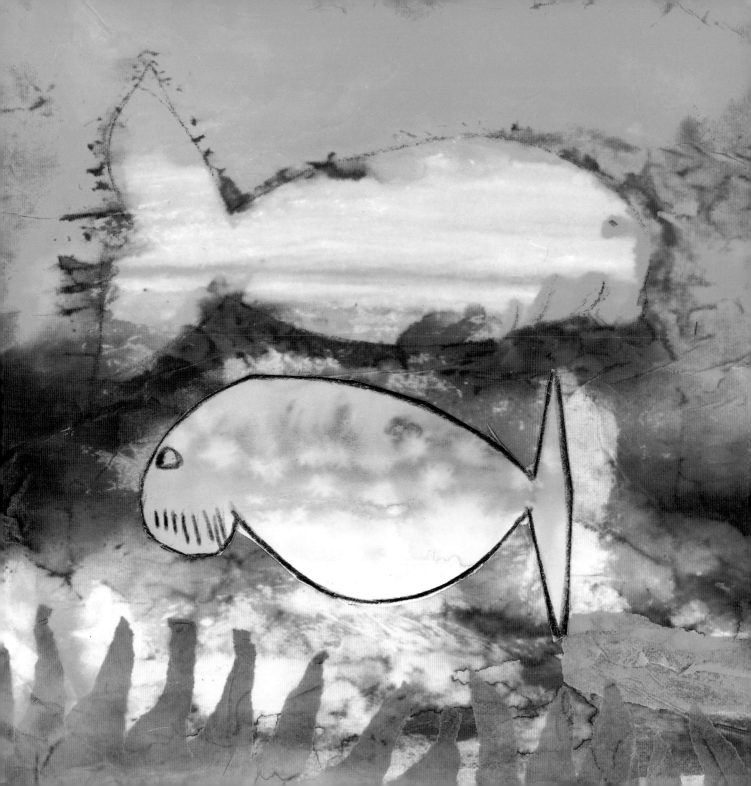

He lunged at an Arntirringa near the shore
but the Arntirringa said,
'No way, Yirrikipayi!
You're not eating me today.
I'm far too jelly
to be in your belly.'

Arntirringa - Jellyfish

He chased a Kirimpika through the mangroves
but the Kirimpika said,
'No way, Yirrikipayi!
You're not eating me today.
I'm too quick and snappy,
I'll make you unhappy.'

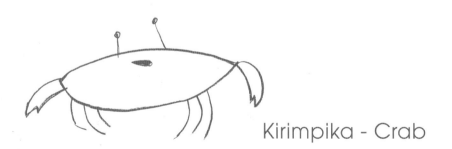

Kirimpika - Crab

Yirrikipayi was sick of chasing troublesome
creatures in the ocean so he headed inland.

He found a Jarrangani in the mud
but the Jarrangani said,
'No way, Yirrikipayi!
You're not eating me today.
I'm too tough and strong,
I'll make you feel wrong.'

Jarrangani – Buffalo

He just missed a Jipwajirringa amongst the long grass

but the Jipwajirringa said,

'No way, Yirrikipayi!

You're not eating me today.

I'm lumpy and jumpy,

I'll make you feel grumpy.'

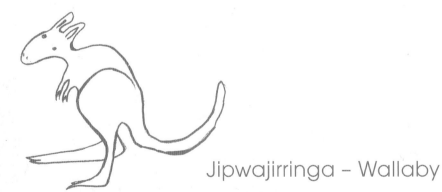

Jipwajirringa – Wallaby

He snapped at a Pika beside the bush
but the Pika said,
'No way, Yirrikipayi!
You're not eating me today.
I'm too strong and fast,
you'll always come last.'

Pika - Horse

He nearly caught a Nyarringari just past the swamp

but the Nyarringari said,

'No way, Yirrikipayi!

You're not eating me today.

I'm too loud and honky,

I'll make you feel wonky.'

Nyarringari - Magpie Goose

Finally, Yirrikipayi grabbed a huge Taringa under a log.

He thought he had his dinner.

But the Taringa coiled around him,

squeezed tight, and said,

'No way, Yirrikipayi!

You're not eating me today.

I'm hungry too

so I'm eating YOU!'

And the Taringa ate Yirrikipayi up.

Taringa - Snake

Finally, Yirrikipayi grabbed a huge Taringa under a log.

He thought he had his dinner.

But the Taringa coiled around him,

squeezed tight, and said,

'No way, Yirrikipayi!

You're not eating me today.

I'm hungry too

so I'm eating YOU!'

And the Taringa ate Yirrikipayi up.

Taringa - Snake

About the Book

Milikapiti Community is situated on the northern coast of Melville Island, one of two islands that make up the Tiwi Islands. The 500 people that live in the community speak mainly Tiwi and English. The local school, with an enrolment of around 80 children, is built only metres from the sea and overlooks a bay which provided much of the inspiration for this story.

In August 2014, the Indigenous Literacy Foundation visited Milikapiti School with a group of ambassadors, including award-winning author and illustrator Alison Lester, to facilitate workshops with the school children.

A group of Middle Years students, along with some local Tiwi assistant teachers, worked with Alison for a whole day. She ran writing and illustrating workshops. As a result, the group wrote and illustrated their very own story, *No Way Yirrikipayi!*, a humorous, clever and catchy story about a hungry crocodile.

In May 2015 Alison travelled back to Milikapiti School to finalise the book. This time, she helped a group of budding artists from across the school learn different art techniques and they created the final illustrations.

The Literacy Production Centre at Murrupurtiyanuwu Catholic School translated the story into Tiwi, the first language of the students. With permission, this book incorporates the Tiwi names of all the animals featured in the story.

This book was made possible with the support of Alison Lester, the Teaching Principal, Suzanne Brogan, staff and students of Milikapiti School.

About ILF

The Indigenous Literacy Foundation is proud to publish *No Way Yirrikipayi!* Our Foundation aims to make a positive difference in the lives of Australian Aboriginal and Torres Strait Islander children by focusing on ways to improve their literacy levels. We believe that a young child's future educational experiences can be greatly improved through enjoyable and positive engagements with books in the family and community environment at an early age.

First published in 2015 by the Indigenous Literacy Foundation
PO Box 663 Broadway NSW 2007

Copyright © for the story, illustrations and photographs remains with the authors.

The moral rights of the authors have been asserted.

Cataloguing-in-Publication details are available from the National Library of Australia

www.trove.nla.gov.au

ISBN 9780992478070

Typesetting and design by Lisa White
Production by Alex Gonzalez
Printed by 1010 Printing International Limited, China